Donald Y. Stewart

First Daily Companion

Of Donald Y. Stewart 1880

Donald Y. Stewart

First Daily Companion
Of Donald Y. Stewart 1880

ISBN/EAN: 9783337300456

Printed in Europe, USA, Canada, Australia, Japan

Cover: Foto ©Andreas Hilbeck / pixelio.de

More available books at **www.hansebooks.com**

DONALD Y STEWART

FIRST DAILY COMPANION

1880

Prepared by Diane Cook

Transcribed by Colleen Thurgood

2009

Family Group Sheet

Husband: John Stewart

Born: June 16, 1810	in: Kallin, Grimsay Island, North Uist, Scotland
Married: Abt. 1830	in: Loch Maddy, North Uist, Inverness, Scotland
Father: Charles Stewart	
Mother: Margaret MacDonald	

Wife: Mary MacLeod

Born: 1811	in: Loch Maddy, North Uist, Scotland
Died: May 07, 1864	in: Framboise, Richmond Co., Nova Scotia
Father: Capt. John MacLeod	
Mother: Mary MacIntosh	

CHILDREN

1	Name: Charles Stewart	
	Born: February 15, 1834	in: Loch Maddy, Invernesshire, Scotland
	Died: October 03, 1902	
M	Married: March 15, 1859	in: Grand River Presbyterian
	Spouse: Jane McDonald	
	Married: October 02, 1887	in: Presbyterian Church , Sydney, Nova Scotia
	Spouse: Anne McDonald	
2	Name: John Stewart	
M	Born: Abt. 1836	
	Died: 1861	in: Framboise,CB,NS
3	Name: Neil Stewart	
	Born: Abt. 1838	in: North Uist, Scotland
M	Died: October 04, 1924	in: Roxbury, MA, USA
	Married: March 25, 1864	in: Grand River, Nova Scotia
	Spouse: Catherine McLeod	
4	Name: Margaret Stewart	
	Born: May 1842	in: Marie Joseph in Framboise, Cape Breton, Nova, Scotia
F	Died: March 16, 1920	
	Married: March 14, 1865	in: Framboise, Richmond County, NS
	Spouse: Ewen MacKenzie	
5	Name: James A. Stewart	
	Born: August 1844	
M	Died: May 24, 1902	in: Oakland, CA
	Married:	
	Spouse: Annie	
6	Name: Alexander Stewart	
	Born: July 16, 1845	in: Framboise, Richmond Co., Nova Scotia
	Died: June 05, 1927	in: Boston, MA
M	Married: Abt. 1870	
	Spouse: Flora	
	Married: July 31, 1897	in: Boston, MA
	Spouse: Christie McKay	
7	Name: Donald Y. Stewart	
	Born: September 02, 1847	in: Framboise, Cape Breton, Nova Scotia
	Died: June 01, 1921	in: St Peters, Richmond Co., Nova Scotia
M	Married: March 14, 1876	in: Grand River, Nova Scotia
	Spouse: Isabella McLeod	
	Married: February 28, 1889	in: St. Peters Presbyterian
	Spouse: Mary Margaret Morrison	
8	Name: Mary Ann Stewart	
	Born: Abt. 1850	in: Framboise, Richmond Co., Nova Scotia
F	Died: Abt. 1930	

1

Family Group Sheet

8	
	Married: March 24, 1874	in: Framboise, Richmond County
F	Spouse: Roderick J. McLean

9	
	Name: Margrette Flora Stewart
	Born: October 14, 1854	in: Framboise, CB. Nova Scotia
F	Died: January 14, 1930	in: Oakland, Alameda County, CA
	Married: July 29, 1873	in: Mira Gut, Cape Breton Co., Nova Scotia
	Spouse: Parmenas Howard Spencer

Family Group Sheet

Husband: Donald Y. Stewart

Born: September 02, 1847 in: Framboise, Cape Breton, Nova Scotia
Married: March 14, 1876　　in: Grand River, Nova Scotia
Died: June 01, 1921　　in: St Peters, Richmond Co., Nova Scotia
Father: John Stewart
Mother: Mary MacLeod
　　Other Spouses:　Mary Margaret Morrison

Wife: Isabella McLeod

Born: November 15, 1853 in: L'ardoise Highlands, Richmond Co., Nova
　　　　　　　　　　　　　　　Scotia
Died: June 14, 1880　　in: Forchu, Richmond Co., Nova scotia
Father: John McLeod
Mother: Mary MacKay

CHILDREN

1 M	Name: John Angus Stewart Born: October 03, 1877 in: L'Archeveque or Fourchu, Richmond 　　　　　　　　　　　　　County NS Died: June 10, 1960　　in: Toronto, Ontario Married: August 27, 1907　in: Cleveland Presbyterian Spouse: Bessie N.R. Morrison Married: 1919 Spouse: Rhoda Gladys Jean Smith
2 F	Name: baby girl Stewart Born: March 1880　　in: Forchu, Richmond Co., Nova scotia Died: June 1880　　in: Forchu, Richmond Co., Nova scotia

Family Group Sheet

Husband: Donald Y. Stewart

Born: September 02, 1847   in: Framboise, Cape Breton, Nova Scotia
Married: February 28, 1889   in: St. Peters Presbyterian
Died: June 01, 1921   in: St Peters, Richmond Co., Nova Scotia
Father: John Stewart
Mother: Mary MacLeod
    Other Spouses: Isabella McLeod

Wife: Mary Margaret Morrison

Born: June 21, 1866   in: St Peters, Richmond Co., Nova Scotia
Died: March 14, 1945   in: St. Peters, Richmond Co., Nova Scotia
Father: Roderick G. Morrison
Mother: Sarah McAskill

CHILDREN

1 M	Name: Roderick Gillivary Stewart Born: December 13, 1890 in: St Peters, Nova Scotia Died: August 08, 1954 in: St Peters, Nova Scotia Married: September 16, 1919 in: St Peters, Nova Scotia Spouse: Annie Mary Hill MacKenzie
2 M	Name: James Gordon Stewart Born: December 25, 1893 in: St Peters, NS Died: 1970 in: NY, NY Married: July 14, 1915 Spouse: Rena Ross Married: September 20, 1922 Spouse: Margaret Ruth MacDonald
3 M	Name: Walter Blair Stewart Born: October 31, 1896 in: St Peters, Richmond Co., Nova Scotia Died: May 1981 Married: December 28, 1922 in: Reno, Nevada Spouse: Alice Meffley
4 F	Name: Mary Isabel Stewart Born: 1898 in: St Peters, Richmond Co., Nova Scotia Died: 1901 in: St Peters, Richmond Co., Nova Scotia

Aug 10 1880

Five years ago last March I could see a bright future before me little thinking of the obscure clouds that were soon to blight my future happiness. It was in those happy days that I examine the only woman I loved. She was the bright flower in her father's house, esteemed by all who had any acquaintance with her. She had many friends and no enemies.

Shortly after our union, troubles began. She was for some months confined to her room in a state of despondency through weak nerves. Finally she got well and we again lived very happily together for over two years. During that time a son was born to us and he inherits the kindness of his mother so far and two years or so afterwards that much dreaded malady "consumption" began to show itself in Mrs. Stewart.

I procured medicine and medical aid for her from far and wide but alas no better and from the first day of June of this year for the space of six weeks she was totally rendered unable to do any kind of work. How be it on the 14th of February 1880 a dear little girl was born and for the space of a week after the baby's birth the mother was getting better all the time and every heart was glad that she would be well again and especially mine but – ah! Soon after, she was getting worse all the time. Then I could see clearly that soon we must part never to meet again on this earth but I always prayed that we should meet again in glory. In her later days when she got weak she could not bear to have me out of sight. She knew that death was near and on the 14th of June 1880 I sadly watched her breathe her last breath pen cannot describe my feelings and my sadness during her long sickness and finally death. All this time the baby was thriving well first under the care of the Grandmother in my own house for six weeks. The Grandmother went home. Then the child was nursed kindly for one month by Mrs. McNeil in her own house and although I amply rewarded her for her kind deed it was much against her will to take any recompense whatever, then the child's aunt, my Sister-in-law Sarah McLeod, through the great kindness and worthiness of her uncle D. McKay Esq. came and took the dear little baby with the intention of raising the child up to womanhood and then return her to me again. I thought I would be happy yet when the boy and girl would grow up but my anticipation were soon again frustrated and more sorrow added to my already big store for on the 26 of June twelve days after her mother's death, the dear baby died. The dear baby died at Lacheveque when she was 3 months and 12 days and was buried aside the mother at Framboise.

It was then I made up my mind (when Bella died) to break house keeping. I kept house very near two months after my wife died, for I had all this troublesome time, a good servant girl Reachel Ferguson. The little boy loved her dearly and my brother lived in the house with me all along and I left him there when I came away. The little boy "John Stewart Angus" was taken to his new home Lacheveque a fortnight before I left. He is

1

driving other more valuable thoughts out of my mind. But if I never see him in this world I trust the Lord has something good and remarkable in store for him to do. The loss of the other two deepened my love for him, then again I would be thinking because your heart is set so much on him the Lord will take him from you but I say let the Lord's will be done in this matter as well as others. He took a dearer one from me and he gave me strength to bear it patiently.

So I left my home in Forchu on the 9th of Aug amidst the tears of my brothers and friends. I called on some closer friends on the way and came to Lacheveque that night. My little boy was delighted to see me. I stopped these two days, went to see a few friends then on the 11th Aug I made my final start from Lacheveque to St. Peters in company with Mr. McKay. I always dreaded that hour to come when I should have to tear myself away from my boy. It came and passed away and I had to bear it.

The ride to St. Peters was very good. The talk and company going over drove a good deal of the loneliness away. I stopped in St. Peters that night at Mr. Norman McLeod. I enjoyed the ride next day to the Straits very much for there was a good gang of his on the stage and many a funny word passed on the journey. Some of those funny folks that we heard on the Stage and going to Boston were Reachel Ferguson, Reachel McLeod, Jessie McLeod and Donald McLeod, the two later were never from home and helped the amusement much more. We stopped a night in the Gut in a very funny house the other gang that was going with us called it the Barrel house. We took the Boston boat next morning Aug 13th. There was a great crowd in her, many the good crowd that was going up to Boston with me was D. McLeod, Archy McLeod, Will McLeod, Donald Ferguson, Donald Matheson and Rory McLeod all going to work for Munro that is the men. We got to Halifax Saturday morning Aug 14th the whole crowd went a shore. Some to see this one and that one and at 4 pm we sailed again for Boston. It was very foggy during the passage at 10 o'clock Monday morning Aug 16th we sighted Boston highland and one hour after we were in port moored fast to II Wharf but I tell you there was a crowd of anxious friends on the wharf waiting to greet us. The first man I knew among the crowd was John Patterson when I landed on the wharf I saw them all. Brother Sandy was there to meet me but I believe there was none more happy to see me than my old shipmate John Morrison. I had to go and take a glass of beer with them and then we all went up to brother Alick. Boston was not to me what it once was once for reasons I will not give here but some may perhaps understand. I went to work in Boston the next day with Ewen McLeod for Munro. I worked two days in Boston and went to New York in company with John McKinnon Aug 18th evening. We took the Fall River line from the cars to one of their floating palaces that from New York to fall ? We got to New York next morning at about nine o'clock and where we landed at pier 28 North River. The baggage men and runners were in herds often to get to take our luggage but we gave them the slip and started. We went straight to the office of George Munro for employment. Munro was not home at the time. His son could not give us any definite answer until the father and chief manager was home but they told us to be there the next day at 7 o'clock and they would send us to work in the vicinity of the city until such time as the Old Munro would be home but before I left the office I called for my old friend John Munro doing work in another department. He was right glad to see me and nothing would do but I would have to got to his house and stay there till such time as I would leave New York. I was right, right glad to go there, but I thought of course that he would charge. I was there four days and when I offered him his money he scorned at it and would not take a cent. His mistress is nothing behind him in benevolence and kindness. I will never forget John Munro's kindness. However the next we went to the office as we were told and both me and John McKinnon were sent out to a place in New Jersey called Patterson about 15 miles from New York. It was a little town of about 20 thousand inhabitants, it is full of factories of all kinds but the chief factories there are woollen and silk factories. We done our work manfully that day and returned to New York that night after distributing 3000 Fireside Specials. The next day we were sent down to a town to a town in Long Island called Flushing about 15 miles from New York. Its inhabitants are about 10 thousand. It is one of the nicest places in Long Island. The most that lives there are rich folk from New York. This was on Saturday Aug 21. Munro came home that day and left orders in the office for me and John to stop there Monday until he would come. We were paid Saturday for the time we worked. I was paid at the rate of $10.00 a week and he was paid at a dollar a day. John did not like this but I could not help him. He was working just as hard as I was. Monday morning we went to the office and the old millionaire was there. He took John in to the office first and in about 10 minutes he came out and was sent to a place near New York a small town called Yanker about ten miles off and finally my turn came to go in the office. I was called in he asked me a few questions gave me $40.00 cash with orders to come to Louisville.

This was Aug 23

I got ready as soon as I could and left New York that evening en route for here. I left my chest in Boston. I left some of my clothes at John Munro's. I only took a valise with me out here. My fare cost me $19.00 but under other circumstances would cost me $22.00. We were going all that night and before morning we were out of the state of New Jersey and in New York again. This day Aug 24 we passed through fine residences and corn plantations. Toward evening we left New York State behind and plunged in the northern part of the State of Pennsylvania. There I saw about 500 of those petrol ion oil tanks studded in the mountains and in the plains here and there of which I often read at home and in the evening I changed cars at station in Pennsylvania called Salamanca. 413 miles from New York and about 150 miles to the south of Niagara Falls.

Louisville Ky

I jumped out of the cars and had a hasty lunch and took another train for Cincinnati, Ohio. We were going through the State of Ohio all that evening and that night until 7 o'clock next day. I changed cars again in Cincinnati about 25 minutes after 7 morning Aug 25 for Louisville, Ky. By this time I was just as black and as dirty with dirt and dust as could be. We came through several tunnels between Cincinnati and Louisville, Kentucky is a fine country. I saw a great many of those old fashioned log houses in Kentucky. I forgot to state the distance between Salamanca and Cincinnati being 448 miles and the distance between Cincinnati and Louisville is 110 miles leaving the distance to New York 971 miles. When I got to Louisville I went at once to the Freight Station of the Indian Star Line and there was 30 thousand Fireside Specials there for me sent out from Munro previous to my crossing. I then got a hotel shewen me by an official in the depot. I went to my hotel at once and washed up left my valise there and went in search of a man to distribute papers with me. I got one in the livery office. After dinner we got to work and that evening I had one bundle Specials distributed.

Aug 25-26 Thursday Aug 26. I put out 3 bundles every bundle holds one thousand.

Aug 27 I put out 3 more bundles put one paper in each house and giving a paper now and then to a man on the street. I wrote to RG McLean today also to James to California.

Saturday Aug 28 I distributed today only two bundles. It rained very heavy in the afternoon with heavy thunder and lightning, much heavier than the thunder in C.B. The north end of the city is infested with Dutch and large pork houses. I think the one third of the population are Negroes. I wrote to John Munro today to Brooklyn.

Sunday 29 I went to church in the Presbyterian tabernacle in Broadway one of the finest churches in America one would be struck at the beautiful workmanship all around her. The minister preached from the 26th ch Acts. The three tunes they sung was Mornington Service and Mozart, they sung the Sanke Hymns. I went in the evening to the Baptist church the preacher was very eloquent, he preached James 16 ch "Acts". A great many of the shops were open today especially grog shops. Letter sent to John Munro.

Louisville

Monday 30th I felt very smart and healthy commenced work right early under a scorching sun and we distributed today 3 1/2 bundles or 3500 papers. We go in the Factories and even gave a paper to an Irishman today and told him to put it in his pocket and read it at night "no he said I'll put it in my hat where all the leuses are". We meet with many peculiar beings all day. When I came home this evening I felt very tired, had supper, shortly after I was taken sick at my stomach. I did not sleep till midnight after relieving my stomach of its contents. Population of Louisville Ky 111,000. One week with Munro.

Tuesday Aug 31

I felt very sluggish this morning for work however I started. After I worked a while I felt better we put 2 1/2 bundles out today it was very hot all day we went through a large Brinly Plow factory. There are about one hundred men working there, everyone at his own post. They were all glad to see us coming to them with reading matter. I got a registered letter from George Munro today containing $20.00. I am just half through put-out – what paper I had today. My board averages about $3.50 a week. I am in a good decent house, nice people. I have to write Munro a postal card every day to report my doings.

4

Sept 1, 1880

I feel pretty tired this evening after working all day in the hot sun. I put out 3 bundles
Special Fireside today. I visited several large factories today but the one that took my
attention most was a Glassery where all kinds of bottles are made. The process is very
simple, when once the mould is made, although it often puzzled me how bottles were ?
Then I went through a large foundry where all kinds of stoves and castings are made, also
a car Factory, also a large stone mill. There all manner of stones are sawed in sheets. I
did not get any letters since I came here from any of my friends. I wrote Brother Charles
today. I feel better this evening.

Sept 2 1880

This day I went to work with a good will as I told Munro I would be done here about
Thursday but at 10 o'clock it rained very heavy for over 3 hours today. I went through
one of the largest Tobacco factories in America. The manager told me they had
customers from Maine to California. I got a good tip from one if the boys. "Give me a
paper Mister is the cry all around me all day from the Street gaffers".

I wrote to Ewen MacKenzie and Donald Cleaves today. Also I sent a paper to Big John
N's son, Donald, Sandy, Dan McKay Esq. and Henry Severance. A great railroad Circus
is expected here tomorrow. Letter sent to Ewen McKay and cleared. This factory was
burned down a few days afterward.

Sept 3 1880

I done pretty well today. I distributed under scorching sun three bundles of Special.
There is a large railroad circus here today, one from Europe and one from California,
Sells Brothers and Shand. It is the biggest procession I ever saw no less than one
hundred large wagons on ambulances. They worked through the city and I was at the
Showground with Specials and I saw the camels, the elephants and the lions and horses
about 30 inches high and monkies riding them. I saw also the great gorilla, they had, the
hippopotamus, then all kinds of trained wild beasts but I did not see them for I did not go
inside the tent. There was thousands of people there from all quarters. The weather is
pretty warm. I am in pretty fair health today. I am anxious to get letters from home.

Sept 4, 1880

I started this morning to go to the west end of the town on Portland Ave. and when I got
out there on the street cars it was a worthless place. So I crossed the Ohio with my man
for a nickel a piece and went up to a little town on the bank of the river called New
Albany. It is in the State of Indiana. I distributed my bundles there to a good advantage
it is full of factories. There is one glass works, there where 500 men works mostly
lowland Scotch and English. I had my picture taken with the bundle on my back. I got a
no letter from home as yet. A fine large Suspension Bridge one mile long spans across
the Ohio River between Louisville and Jeffersonville, Indiana.

Sept 5, Sunday

I felt very miserable all day from a pain in the back opposite my kidneys. I did not go to church at all. I enjoyed the Sunday pretty much in my room but it is awful what noise and hustle there is outside.

Sept 6 Monday

I did not feel very willing to go to work today as the pain in my back was just as bad in the morning. It rained about 2 hours in the morning, so I did not go out till about 9 o'clock. I got an express to take 4 bundles up to 19th St. and when I got fairly to work I felt much better. So I am better this evening, we visited several factories today a large plow and furniture factory. I was in the post office and no letter from home yet. I will have 30 bundles put out since I came here. Two weeks at $10.00 per week.

Sept 7, 1880

This morning I went to work pretty early to the western part of Louisville City. I put out 1500 Specials before dinner but we had to work pretty hard as the houses were very few and far between. Then we came home on the horse cars, had dinner. Then I went to Jeffersonville with the last bundle I had on hand. I got through these all right. Jeffersonville is on the western side of the Ohio River in the State of Indiana. I paid off my man tonight until I get a new lot. I feel very tired today my back aches but not quite so bad. I have a Capicine plaster on it. I find this to be very hard work so far but the climate has taken a change for the colder. I slept all day till last night with nothing but a sheet over me.

Sept 8, 1880

I am idle today waiting for orders from George Munro. I have nobody to keep me company but sit down and think of the past and what is to become of me. I dread to say I have a nasty cough but perhaps it is from the cold I had a few days ago but then I feel a kind of aching pain in my back and sometime in my breast but I hope it will not come to what I dread.

Sept 9

I am idle today also but my pay is going on all the same. Although I would sooner work. I had a letter from John Munro today and it was very acceptable being the first I got from a friend since I came here. I do not know what minute my orders will come from Munro for to go some where. I wrote to Sarah McLeod today and sent my picture to Jonny Angus. I feel a little better today. The cough is leaving me. It is very fine weather here now. I generally go to bed between seven and eight. I don't go around anywhere. It is one month today since I left Forchu.

Sept 10

I passed this day idle with regards to work like the two succeeding ones. I pass most of the time in my room reading. There was a great fire here this morning in a large Tobacco factory it was completely destroyed but plenty more of them in the city. I feel pretty well today. Wrote Henry Severance today and to Achy MacLeod and John Munro N.Y.

Sept 11

This is the fourth day I am idle. I would sooner work for I pass my time very lonely. I am eagerly looking for letters from home but they don't seem to come. I did not get a word from James as yet but I may be thankful to God that my health is returning to me again. Tomorrow the commissionaire will be at Framboise. I would like to be there poor Bella was with me the last one them but I hope she sits at a higher banquet now. I made nine cigars tonight of leaf tobacco. Wrote brother Sandy sent paper to H. Soverance.

Sept 12 Sunday

I have spent the most of this day in my room reading, meditating. Church bells are ringing in all directions but the noise and hustle on the streets almost deadens the church bells. At ½ past 8 pm I went to the Broadway Tabernacle the text was from Matthew 26 ch 39 verse. The singing was beautiful.

Monday Sept 13

I am now idle for near a week and I went this morning to the post office with the expectation of hearing from Munro but no answer. I am getting weary of being idle. No letter from home yet. Evening got a telegram from Munro stating that he sent me registered letter Sept 4. I showed the telegram to the postmaster, he overhauled all the letters, the answer was "no letter" but as the telegram states (must be in the office). He overhauled the books and found that there was one but was forwarded to Indianapolis. I telegraphed for it at once. As I was in a strait for money to pay my way. I knew Munro must have wrote although I telegraphed him the facts and wrote him also, received telegram from Munro 3 pm. Third week.

Seymour, Ind- Sept 14

This day I got the long expected letter from Munro containing $20.00 and as the train on which I was to leave for Seymour Ind was not going till 2:55 pm I had 4 hours to spare. So I thought I would visit the great Exposition now held at Louisville. I got in for 25 cents and it was a good investment as I saw a great many things worth seeing there. I saw a sample of all kinds of goods manufactured in the United States. I cannot describe everything, all kinds of grain, cotton hardware, dry goods a specimen of everything I could think of. But one wonderful thing I saw was a Mammoth Elephant, 18 ft high and 26 ft long, stuffed, his legs were as large as a large tree the freight of it from Europe, cost 860 dollars. I cannot tell all in this short page however I left it came to the depot in time for the train. I came to Seymour, Indiana where I am writing this now. I stop at the Opera Hotel. I am well in health. I am going to bed now. Fare from Louisville to Seymour $2.25. Population of Seymour 2372. DY Stewart

Columbus, Ind- Sept 15

I went to work at Seymour this morning right fresh after being so long idle. I distributed 700 Specials. It is a nice little town on the Louisville and Indianapolis road. I got through them about 10 am then I started for Northern Vernon a branch 16 miles off and as I was getting my bundles off the engine to put them in the caboose I jumped off bullgine and sprained my foot very bad. I could hardly walk but by time I got to Vernon I was a little better but found it very hard to walk. The doctor gave me liniment to rub it with however I got through at Vernon and came on here to Columbus. I stop at the Sident Hotel. This is a fine country very level, not a stone, a yellow sandy grain. The board is higher in hotels in Indiana than in Kentucky. Fare from Seymour to North Vernon 45 cents, from Vernon to Columbus 85 cents, population Columbus 2359.

Edinburgh, Ind- Sept 16

I came here this morning from Columbus after distributing 1 bundle Specials. This, the finest farms I have seen yet is between Edinburgh and Columbus just as level as the floor. I got to this place in a caboose attached to a freight train. I am stopping here in the Galt House. I am in the best room I was in since I left home for the same price. I have only 500 Specials out here. My foot is much better tonight. Fares Columbus to Edinburgh 50 cents. Population of Columbus 1499.

Sept 17

I came to Franklin today at 9 am I distributed the papers all right there and I then went to Country Fair now held here. I paid a quarter to get in and I was delighted to know that two horse races was coming off as I went in to the grounds. A running race and a trotting race continued on the side. Edinburgh to Franklin 40 cents. Population of Franklin 2707.

It was the finest thing ever I saw. I thought the grey horse was pretty fair till I saw them. Three on each race best-out-of three one mile heat they were like the wind. Best time they made trotting 2 minutes and 50 seconds and the running horse mile in two minutes. So that they can hardly be beat. There was about 5000 men there exhibiting every kind of produce and every kind of farming implements but I did not look much at the farming materials for I was on the race course all the time. I long to get to Indianapolis for I know that I have lots of letters there. I will try and be there tomorrow, Saturday. Fare from Franklin to Shelbyville 75 and Shelbyville to Indianapolis $100.

Indianapolis, Ind. Population 100,000- Sept 18

I came here this evening 7pm from Shelbyville, Ind. There was a great political campaign in Shelbyville all day by the democrats but when I got here there was a tremendous republican campaign. Here it is nine pm now and thousands are walking and parading the street all in uniforms. The democratic nominee is Hancock for president and English for Vice Pres and the Republican Nominees are Garfield for president and Arthur for Vice Pres. There is a very hot contest between them and dangerous to walk the streets. I am tonight in James Hotel. I was very disappointed when I went to the post office after I came. It was closed and I know I have letters from home there. I could get them tomorrow (Sunday) but I will not go. DY Stewart

Indianapolis- Sept 19th Sunday

I did not go to church today for I did not know where to go this is a wicked city. I came here Saturday night. I am in my room most all the time for it is disgusting to hear such nasty language going on. There is no thought of eternity or death in this part of the world at all.

Monday 20

I went to the post office today making sure I had letters from home but no letters. It seems when I am out of sight I am out of mind. I got the bundles all right (16). I put two bundles out today. I got a registered letter from Munro containing $20.00. This is a fine clean city. I get good board all along. I have good appetite so far. I am in pretty good health. 4 weeks with Munro.

Indianapolis- Sept 21

This day I worked without a boy the first part of it and after working very hard I only distributed 2 1/2 bundles. This city is much harder to pass papers than Louisville, Ky. I don't like this town at all it is full of Music and Sport night and day. There are 4 doctors in a pavilion opposite my window lecturing about medicine every night and between every speech they sing, play the fiddle and organ and act. The Irishman, Dutchman and the one from the firm of Hammel and Lewis Chicago. I bought a package of Catarrh remedy from them to send to Sandy. Fine, healthy weather here now. I never got a word from any of my friends yet whether they are dead or alive, they don't imagine how I feel.

Indianapolis- Sept 22

Today I am bent on working hard to see if I could distribute 3 bundles and I did so under great difficulty. I have a new boy every day and I have so much trouble to learn them. The Soldiers Mioco have a big time in the city today firing cannons and walking through the town.

9

Sept 23

I worked pretty hard today I am very tired tonight. I put out almost 3 bundles. I saw great sight today the Soldiers had a sham battle in the Fair grounds. It was a good sight to see. I am almost deaf from the cannons firing. I got a letter from Munro today and $20.00 cash being $100.00 I got from him for my expense line. I left New York but no letters from home yet.

Indianapolis- Sept 24

I worked hard today. I put out 21/2 bundles today. I will soon be done in this town and I am very glad of it. My next route is to Greencastle, Terre Haute, Vincennes, Princetown, Evansville, Ind. and back again to Louisville Ky. I am grieved that I don't get a letter from home. Wrote to James today.

Sept 25 (Saturday)

I feel pretty tired after my days work but my health is good so far. I went through today a large wagon Factory employing 450 men. I never saw such a sight on carriages before. I was also through a large rolling Mill employing over 300 men. Also I was through a Saw Factory where all kinds of saws are made. I will leave here on Monday. I am done here but one bundle, 2 bundles today. DY Stewart

Indianapolis- Sept 26

They have fine churches from the outside here and I think that is all what they look for. I did not get to any church twice. I left Louisville. I stopped in my room all day there is a hand case in the room with me.

Sept 27- Greencastle, Ind

I came this afternoon after finishing Indianapolis and when I got here there was no bundle for me here and it must go astray for Munro notified me that it was here. The great State fair and Exposition commences today at Indianapolis. I wrote Neil the second letter today. I am well thank God, I have good appetite. I stop at the Union Hotel. DY Stewart. Five weeks with Munro. Fare from Indianapolis to Greencastle $1.20.

Terre Haute Ind.- Sept 28

I finished Greencastle as good as could be and then came on here in 2 pm train. The bundle I spoke of yesterday came this morning from Indianapolis. I got the bundle here all right (5 in number). This is a thriving little town full of Factories of every kind. When I came in here I went to hotel and I found out afterwards that it was a den of thieves. I made an excuse and I now stop at the Exchange House $1.00 per day. Green Castle to Terre Haute $10.55.

Sept 29

I worked hard today feel very sore, this is a fine little city. I was in a large rolling mill today making every kind of iron works. The population of this town is about 20,000. I like this house very well. There is a large, fine bar attached but very little of my nickels will go that way. Fine high living every where I go but I would sooner have potatoes and herring sometimes than all them dainties. DYS Sent 2 papers to H. Severance.

Sullivan, Ind.- Sept 30

This part of the States is more civilized. Nice people from what I have seen in the rest of the States and for the first time since I left New York. I stop in a private house tonight and I like it well. I finished Terre Haute today came here at 5pm. I will be down here tomorrow only. I am then going to Vincennes, Ind. I began to like the work a little better. I saw a great deal in the cars and see such nice view of the fertile country all around. If I had one more with me that would follow me all the time it would be much better. If Rory Ferguson or Archy MacLeod was with me it would be nice but-no. I am going to bed. I was trying to make nails today in Terre Haute in the nail factory but I could not make one. Fare from Terre Haute to Sullivan $1.00.

Vincennes Ind.- Oct 1, 1880

I got through all Sullivan today early but as there are only a morning and evening train going south I had to wait there all day. I took advantage of being idle and I wrote a long letter to DA McLean and another to Christy McLeod "Mrs. Finlayson". I got here at 5:15 pm. I stop at the Avenue Hotel. Sullivan to Inverness $1.25.

Princeton, Ind.- October 2 (Saturday)

I got here this evening at a little past six. I was through in Vincennes at 3 pm. I had to wait there till 5pm for the Evansville train. This seems to be a nice little town situated on the Evansville and Terre Haute road. Its population is about 4000. I must lay here over Sunday as I have to pass about 400 Specials Monday morning before going to Evansville. I hope I will have letters in Evansville. Good night DY Stewart.

Princeton, Ind.- Sunday Oct 3

I went to the Presbyterian Church this morning the minister preached a very touching sermon from Acts 19 ch and 20 verses. Princeton is a very nice little town, very quiet. I stop at the Gibson Hotel $1.00 per day. Vincennes to Princeton $1.00. Jonny Angus birthday 3 years today.

Oct 4

I got very early at Princeton today so that I would have the papers passed before the 8 o'clock train for Evansville. I got through and was just at the depot as the train was coming in. I jumped on board and came here to Evansville. I went to the post office and behold there was no letter from Munro and I had very little money, however I went to the depot and I got the agent to give me 2 bundles until I would get the money or I would be idle all day, so I passed them off all night. Wrote to Sandy. Six weeks with Munro.

Evansville, Ind.- Oct. 5

I must say that I felt very miserable and greatly disappointed all day as I am, I may say totally out of money. Munro notified me in Indianapolis that a registered letter would be here for me but through some mistake or other it has not come. It looks very blue for me to be here in a place over 1000 miles from any person that would aid me. I feels as if every body I meet knew my circumstances. I do not know what minute the boarding master will want his pay and no money to give and worst still I telegraphed Munro that I was in a Strait for money and no answer came yet-there must certainly be something awry and if I could work I would not feel so bad but I cannot pay the freight on the bundles and therefore cannot get them. Tomorrow maybe better. Fare from Princeton to Evansville $1.00.

Evansville- Oct 6

I was relieved this morning at 8 am from hitherto approved dishes I got $20.00. So I was glad I got to work right off and worked hard all day and put out 3000 Specials. I will leave for Louisville tomorrow if I spared by the 10:15 train. I was overjoyed to get a letter from RJ McLean today which gave me the news of the place. There is a great demonstration and Democratic Campaign here tonight in Honour of Hancock, thousands are walking the streets. Wrote to J. Monro and to J. McLean.

Louisville, Ky- Oct 7

Back to Louisville again. I got to work right-early this morning at Evansville, Ind. as I had only one bundle to distribute and had to catch the 10:15 am train for Louisville via A & M railroad. I got straight in here and started. I was coming all day. I got here at 8:15 pm. The fare cost me $6.00. I stop at the same Hotel. Got a letter from James. Fare from Evansville to Louisville $6.00.

Oct 8

When I went to the depot this morning there was four bundles there for me and 6 more came today. I got a man and went to work and put out 3 bundles. I did not get a letter from Munro since I came here but I was glad as there was a letter for me here from James and when I went to the post office there was another there for me from him that he wrote long ago and I was gone before it came. Wrote to James and Sandy.

Louisville- Oct 9

This day dawned fine as usual. I put out 3 bundles today. I expected a letter from Munro today not letter as yet. I was ever so glad to get letter from home which I expected long ago. I do not know how long I will be here until I get this order from Munro. Got 5 letters from home today, 2 from Sarah McLeod, 1 from Neil, 1 from Charlie from ?, 1 from Kathy and Blair. I wrote Sarah tonight. Two months since I left Forchu.

Oct 10 "Sunday"- I may say I stopped in my room reading all day. The streets are busy and noisy.

Oct 11

I got a registered letter from Munro today containing $30.00. It rains today I cannot work. I wrote to KJ McLean and sent papers to Severance. I would sooner work every day for I feel so dull when I am idle sitting in the Hotel. Everybody seems to be happy but me but I am not displeased for my lot. 7 weeks with Munro.

Louisville, Ky- Oct 12

It rained here this afternoon after dinner it came up fine and I got to work. We went out to the northern outskirts of the city. We put out one bundle, the houses were so scattered. It took all afternoon to canvas them. The State Election for Governor is today held in Indiana. There is a very hot contest between the Democrats and Republicans. A great many are killed and murdered through disputes arising between the parties. The Marshall of Shelbyville and a Negro was shot dead a few days ago by a republican mob. This is a dangerous country to be in. You don't know who is your friend. The second day of Nov. is the day for the Presidential election. Both sides are claiming a victory so far. I am drowsy tonight. I am going to turn in.

Louisville Ky- Oct 13

This day broke forth radiant and fine. I commenced to work early. I took one bundle out to ?? before dinner. It took us all the forenoon to distribute that as the houses were so far apart. We visited Phoenix brewery because many worked there. We could get all the beer we wanted for nothing but we did not drink but very little. After dinner we went out South on Preston St. and put one more bundle out there in the afternoon. I think we walked over 16 miles today. The Republicans gained the day in Indiana. They claim 2500 majority for Porter but the returns are not all in they will know the exact figure tomorrow. DY Stewart

Louisville Ky- Oct 14

I went to work right early this morning. I worked about ½ hour. It rained and thundered. So I did not finish the last bundle till the afternoon. I have no more bundles until a new supply comes. Full report of election came in. Republicans majority over

13

7000, they are jubilant over it. I sent a paper (courier journal) to Neil a letter enclosed. I sent another paper of the same to Donald McLean, St. Esprit.

Oct 15

It rained very heavy here most all day. I got ten bundles more new Specials from Munro this evening. I left so very unhappy all the week that I felt very miserable but I am better this evening. I think if I was thin before I left home I will be thinner before I leave this place. I am thinking those papers that I am distributing is a great evil and it hurts me to think that I am there agent.

Louisville Ky- Oct 16

This has been a fine cool day, a little cloudy and few drops rain in the morning. I distributed 3 bundles today. I received ten more bundles today in different lots making in all 30 bundles new Specials. Since I came this time to Louisville I distributed to date 15 bundles. I have 17 more bundles on hand tonight. I had a letter from Sandy today. I am glad to hear that he is getting along well now. I will write him tonight.

Oct 17 (Sunday)

This has been a very fine cool day. I don't go to church now at all because they talk (minister) so peculiar and I am dull in hearing so I stop pretty much in my room. I would sooner hear one Sermon down home than all this preaching here. DY Stew

Louisville- Oct 18

This day dawned fine and cold for the time a year. I would not want it any colder than it was today it was just about right for my business. I worked hard today, I distributed 31/2 bundles Specials. I was in a white lead mill today. The white paint is made of lead dissolved by acid covered with tar bash. I expected letters today but got none. Wrote to Kathy A. Blair. 8 weeks with Munro.

Oct 19

It rained a short time this forenoon but I managed to distribute 3 bundles. I received a reg. letter from Munro today giving me orders to go on the same route I was before when I would be done here. I got a letter from Henry Severance today also and I was very glad to hear the news. Wrote to G. Munro and H. Severance.

Oct 20

It was kind of cloudy the first part of the day. I worked very hard this day walking on the pavement. Steady all day with a load on my back most all the time. I put out 31/2 bundles today to a good advantage. I will be done here about the first of next week.

Oct 21

I had a hard job to distribute 21/2 bundles today in western part of the city, the houses were so few and far between. I was in a Shoe Factory today. I saw the way they sew the soles on shoes. I was also in a large Tobacco Factory worked by Finnegan Brothers that got burnt out some time ago. Good night I am going to bed. DY Stewart

Oct 22

I distributed 11/2 bundles today. It rained here in the afternoon. I did not get my letter here but the ones I got when I came here. I went out to Portland with the bundles today and found that there was not houses enough for them so I went across to New Albany with ½ a bundle. Sent papers to H. Severance.

Oct 23

I went this morning across to New Albany, Ind. I distributed two bundles there. I was in the great Glass works there it wonderful how they manage everything so complicated. Window glass is first made in large round tubes then cut length way on one side, then heated over and flayed out in large flat pieces, cooled and then cut in the size. Two months since I left New York.

Oct 24 (Sunday)

This day has been very fine. I stopped in the Hotel most all day there is a convention held here now by all the Ministers of the Christian Church in the United States.

Oct 25

Fine day, I went to Jeffersonville this morning with the last bundle. I got through by eleven o'clock. I am to leave Louisville at 2:55 pm today for Seymour, Ind. Wrote John Munro.

Oct 25- Seymour, Ind.

I arrived at 5 pm from Louisville all safe. I got the bundle here all right. I stop at the Opera House or Wilson Hotel. I am in good health thank God and have pretty fair appetite. Louisville to Seymour $2.25, Seymour to North Vernon, 45cents, North Vernon to Columbus 85 cents. 9 weeks with Munro.

Columbus, Ind.- Oct 26

I arrived here this evening at 5pm from Seymour and North Vernon. I finished Seymour this morning at 10:20 am then took the A & M for North Vernon in a caboose. I took art of the bundle to North Vernon about 400 Specials as the place is much smaller than Seymour. It was dull and cloudy all day, rained very heavy last night. I got a letter today from Cleaves and reg. letter from Munro. Ticket at 50. Letter from Charles.

Edinburgh, Ind- Oct 27

I finished Columbus and came here in a caboose at 3 pm found the bundle paid the freight and distributed a few, the evening weather dull and cold. I board at the same hotel Gall House. DY Stewart   Ticket 40 cents

Shelbyville, Ind.- Oct 28

I went to work this morning at Edinburgh very early. I got through at 8:38 and started for Franklin with the rest of the bundle. I finished Franklin at noon. Now the route I took to Shelbyville before was through Fairland but I could Franklin till tomorrow at 10:30 am and I would not get to Shelbyville till after 4 o'clock in the evening so I thought do the train by Columbus which I did and got here at 6:30 pm ticket by this route $1.80 and by Fairland south 75 cents but I will gain by paying $1.80 for I can work tomorrow and my board at Franklin would be 75 cents. Waiting for the train the reason I got so soon ahead on that route before. There was a freight train behind time in Fairland and I got aboard that. From Franklin to Shelbyville via Columbus $1.80.

Indianapolis- Oct 29

I finished Shelbyville at 11 am. I barely caught the 11:10 train for Indianapolis. I got there a little past noon. I had eleven bundles in the depot and I had 3 letters in the office all from home. I paid the people and will go to work tomorrow. Received letter from Sarah McLean, Christy Finlayson and Ewen McLean. Wrote to Sarah and Parmenus Spencer. Ticket $1.00. ᴍᶜᴸᴱᴬᴰ   ᴹᵃᶜᴳᵃᵐˢᵀ   ᴸᵃᴳᴳɪᴿ.

Oct 30

I got to work early this morning. I distributed 3 1/2 bundles and a catalogue with each paper. It rained a short time at noon but nothing to hard. I am stopping at the same hotel. I have a room for myself now. Wrote to Christy Finlayson and John Munro.

Sunday- Oct 31

This has been a fine day. I passed the most of the day in the room reading.

Nov 1- Indianapolis 1880

Time slips by and winter is approaching there was hoar frost on the ground this morning. I went to work this morning as usual. I worked harder today than I did for a long time and yet I only got out 3 bundles and 9 bunches of catalogues. My feet skinned about the

16

toes for the first time. Tomorrow is Election Day for the President of the United States. 10 weeks with Munro.

Nov 2

I worked pretty hard today as usual. I distributed 3 bundles. The Election came off today but the result is not known as yet but by all appearances Garfield will be elected. I was to several of the polling places and they kept quiet all day but many lost his life thus this campaign and it is now ended. Received reg. letter from Munro.

Indianapolis- Nov 3

I distributed the last of the bundles (21/2) today. I expected 4 more to come but if they are not here tomorrow I am going to Greencastle. This has been a great day here tonight the town is illuminated with rocket and cannons firing and a regular babble of voices. It puts me in mind of a swarm of bees, hum, hum. I care very little about them. I don't go among them at all. The Democrats are crestfallen over their failure. Got a letter from James and wrote James.

Greencastle- Nov 4

As there are no bundles in the depot at Indianapolis this morning I concluded to leave for this place. I arrived here.at 2 pm. I got the bundle and distributed half of it this evening. It rained very heavy this evening. It rained very heavy this morning. I stop at the Union Hotel $1.00 per day. DY Stewart   Sent election papers to PH Spencer, HJ McLean and John Stewart, ?? from Indianapolis. Ticket $1.20 Vandalia line.

Terre Haute, Ind.- Nov 5

This has been a very dull day I finished Greencastle this afternoon and left on the 1:25 pm train to Terre Haute $1.05. I got the bundles here all right. I distributed ½ bundles this evening without a boy. The Election Fever is over now. Sent paper to H Severance.

Nov 6

This has been a very disagreeable day raining and snowing all day and very cold, this has been the first snow here this season. I did not work any today and on that account I felt the day long. Wrote to Archy McLeod.

Sunday- Nov 7

It froze hard last night making ice on the puddles. I did not go to any church. I stopped in the hotel all day every Grog Shop in town is open today as well as other days.

Terre Haute- Nov 8

I worked hard today so that I would be able to go on the morning train tomorrow to Sullivan and Vincennes. I distributed 3 1/2 bundles. I was in the great Nail Factory it is quite a wonder to see how nails are made. One man can make over 100 pound an hour there are about 100 nail feeders in the factory. They will turn out about 1000 casks a day. 11th week with Munro.

Vincennes, Ind.- Nov 9

Finished Terre Haute this morning as early as possible and came to Sullivan. Distributed half bundle then and came here on the last train. I stopped before in the Avenue Hotel but now I stops at the Mitchel House a better hotel for the same money. Looks cloudy and threatening tonight, wind snow and cold. I am in good health now. DY Stewart

Princeton, Ind.- Nov 10

It is five weeks since I was here before. I finished Vincennes today and it was quite a walk for it is a real country town, two houses on a square. However I got through and got these at 8 pm the train was an hour behind time. I am at the Gibson House.

Evansville, Ind.- Nov 11

I finished Princeton right early this morning and came here at 10 o'clock. I got the bundles and letters all right. I had a letter from DA McLean today. I was right glad to get the news from home. I will try hard and finish here tomorrow if I am spared. I have a great deal of trouble in getting boys to help me work.

Evansville, Ind.- Nov 12

I done a big days work here today and I feel pretty sore tonight. I wanted to go to Louisville tonight on 6:25 pm train. I will be there if nothing happens tomorrow morning at 7 o'clock. I distributed 3 1/2 bundles today and I had only a small boy but he was very smart.

Louisville, Ky- Nov 13

I was coming all night from Evansville. I got here at 8 this morning, there was 20 bundles here for me and a lot of letters. I received news from home today that the house and lots in Forchu are to be sold at auction by the Sheriff. Nothing done that but ? I felt miserable all day about it but I know that is nonsense. We have our health and can build again on a better footing. I am tired tonight. 2 bundles today out.

Louisville, Ky- Nov 14

Sunday, fine cold day. I did not go much out all day. I was reading in my room most of the time. People think very little of Sunday here.

Nov 15

It was bitter cold last night and froze quite hard. I found it pretty cold all day distributing papers but I done a good days work. I distributed 3 1/2 bundles. It looks cloudy and dull this evening. I think it will snow. I am in pretty good health now.

Nov 16

Fine cold weather for working. I worked hard today also I distributed 3 1/2 bundles. I got a letter from Band & Co yesterday.

Louisville, Ky- Nov 17

It snowed a couple inches last night and it was bitter cold here all day. I distributed 2 bundles but it was hard to handle them on account of the cold.

Nov 18

It has been desperate cold all day. It snowed about 3 inches last night. We found it very cold this morning, handling papers, however we distributed 3 bundles. Riding sleighs were on the streets all day.

Nov 19

I did not work this forenoon on account of cold drizzling snow. I put out 1 1/2 bundles in the afternoon. Very cold weather here now. I had no letter since I came here but those others were here ahead of me. I am pretty well posted in Louisville now. I know every nook and corner.

Louisville, Ky- Nov 20

This has been a fine day. I distributed 3 bundles streets were wet and muddy. I had a letter from Dan Ferguson from New Orleans today. I went to the post office this evening to post a letter but the delivery office was closed and I was sorry for it for I saw a letter for me in the advertisement list and cannot get it till Monday, if I don't go tomorrow (Sunday) for it.

Nov 21 (Sunday)

I went to the post office this morning to get the letters for I knew they were from home and I could not endure to sit in all day and think about it one from Sarah and one from McLean. I went to the Methodist Church on Broadway the minister, preacher a fine sermon, it is real cold weather.

Louisville, Ky- Nov 22

Fine cold day real frosty. I distributed 21/2 bundles in the southern outskirts of the city. Nothing new on the program.

Nov 23

I had several letters from home today many of them are from Neil, St. Peters telling about the land and lots in Forchu to be sold at auction. This has been a fine cool day. I distributed 2 bundles in the outskirts of the city. I wrote 4 letters this evening. I sent a Telegram to McAuish MPP tonight to purchase the Forchu lots for us.

Nov 24

I did not work any this day on account light but wet snow dripping all day. I had another bundle in the depot this morning containing 10,000 catalogues of the Sea Side library.

Louisville, Ky- Nov 25

It snowed here the better part of last night and all this forenoon so then I did not start till the afternoon as it cleared up about 11 o'clock. I distributed 1 small bundle Specials and 600 catalogues. I was in a large Pork house where they killed hogs at the rate of three a minute.

Nov 26

I was distributing catalogues all the forenoon because it snowed heavy and I could keep them dry in a bag. It cleared about noon. So I distributed one bundle Specials and a lot of catalogues in the afternoon. I sent Telegram to McAuish M.P.P. tonight Mrs. James don't want Forchu lots therefore I cannot buy. So Forchu will soon be occupied by a contemporary.

Nov 27

The sun shone today a while, the first time since a week. I distributed 21/2 bundles between Louisville and Jeffersonville. I bought a pair of shoes tonight (Brogans) $4.50. I had a letter from Henry Severance today. It is much warmer in Cape Breton now than here for they had plenty of snow and ice here and home in Cape Breton yet by what I learn.

Nov 28 (Sunday)

I stayed in the Hotel all day. I was disgusted with some of the boarders they commenced to play checkers all the evening like any other day.

Nov 29

I was over to New Albany today and finished all the Specials I had. I will leave here tomorrow for the same route I had before. ? weeks with Munro.

Seymour, Ind.- Nov 30

I finished Louisville this morning distributing catalogues. I came here on the 2:10 pm and got here at 4 pm but the bundles was not here before me as I thought. There is much more snow here than at Louisville. I saw the ugliest Slay I think in the world here today. An acquaintance of mine Dr. Noyette from Detroit is in the Hotel tonight he was glad to see me.

Dec 1- North Seymour, Ind.

I finished Seymour this evening and came here at 4 pm. I finished here also. I will leave here at 7 am tomorrow. I stop at the Hotel Kelly. I wrote to Sarah today and to Dan Ferguson, New Orleans.

Edinburgh, Ind.- Dec 2

I left North Vernon this morning at 7:10 am, came to Columbus at 8:05 am got three bundles and distributed all by noon. I left in a caboose at 1:30 pm and came here at the Kelly house. He charged me $1.00 for two meals and bed. I will leave here if spared at 8:30 am tomorrow for Franklin. It is freezing tonight. I distributed about 300 Specials this evening

Dec 3- Shelbyville, Ind.

I finished Edinburgh pretty early this morning and came to Franklin. I finished there at 3 pm and left on the 3:48 pm train by the way of Columbus. It cost $1.80 but I will gain after all as I will be a day ahead in Indianapolis. I had quite a job this night to get a hotel as the one I was to stop is closed.

Indianapolis- Dec 4

I am in the town for the third time. I do not know how long I will stay as there are no bundles in the depot for me. I came from Shelbyville this afternoon. I had a letter from John Munro stating that my clothes were coming in a bundle of catalogues.

Dec 5 Sunday

It was pretty cold today. I did not go out hardly any but it is a regular plaque to listen to all the vulgarity and swearing that goes on all day, enough to frighten anybody but there day is coming that will bring all this to light.

Indianapolis- Dec 6

It was very cold here all day. I had a bundle of catalogues with my clothes inside today from New York. I feel quite comfortable now as I have plenty warm clothes for the winter. I expected a letter from Sarah today but none came. I will have some in a few days I think. I distributed ½ bundle and 9 bunches catalogues.

Dec 7

It was extremely cold today mercury showed 7 deg. I worked hard all day. I distributed 15 bunches catalogues. I wrote in a mistake to Munro that I distributed 16 bunches.

Dec 8

I distributed 13 bunches catalogues today under a drifting snow and frost but I had a good man with me. He is a prize pedestrian and won many foot races and is not over 19 years old. He made $800 last week on a walking matter.

Indianapolis, Ind.- Dec 9

I worked pretty hard all day. I distributed 13 bunches catalogues of 250 each. The winter has set in pretty hard here now. I did not get a letter from this last fortnight here.

Dec 10

I got a letter from Sarah today. I was glad to know that they were all well. I distributed the last of the second bundle today which leaves 15,000 catalogues distributed to date. There is another bundle coming. The weather is still cold, very cold.

Dec 11

I was idle today through a mistake of Munro him sending the bundle to the wrong depot and did not notify me but the company sent a card to the post office and I got the bundle in the evening.

Indianapolis - Dec 12 (Sunday)

It thawed some today. I did not go to church. I stopped in the house all day. I had an invitation from a fellow to go to see the inside of the prettiest and costliest house in the city but I did not go.

Dec 13

I worked well today. I distributed 15 bundles catalogues. I will be done of them tomorrow but I will have a shipment of Specials soon and I have to go over the city the second time but I feel bad about 4 bundles that are in the depot since I was here before and I left not knowing that they were there as they were sent by a different line to what I got the other specials. I wrote Munro about it but I did not hear from him yet I don't know what to do with them but it was not my fault. 16 weeks with Munro.

Indianapolis- Dec 14

I finished the last of the catalogues today. I distributed in all in this city 3 bundles on 22,500 catalogues. I was into every house in the city. I have a new lot of Special Fire Side coming on the way. I did not get any letter from James since I came here. I was in a real palace meat market today "Kingen & Co".

Dec 15

Munro sent me a telegram Monday to distribute the old catalogues but it seems it was not mailed till today and I only got it about 1 o'clock today. I immediately went to work and I distributed 11/2 bundles. The new Specials has not arrived yet. I had a letter from Sarah today which was mailed at Lacheveque on the 9th nish only six days coming here. I was glad to hear the news from home.

Indianapolis- Dec 16

This was a fine mild day. I distributed the last of the old Specials being 21/2 bundles. I expect the New Specials to be here at my house so I am ready for them. I wrote James today. I have pretty good times now not much hard work and plenty of good eatables and a good sound sleep at night. So I ought to be thankful to God there I am in health and can enjoy those luxuries.

Dec 17

I have been idle today for want of stock. The bundles were shipped from New York on the 11insh and should have been here yesterday but has not arrived as yet. I am going to bed. It is nearly eight o'clock and I will have a long sleep before seven tomorrow. I am yours etc etc **DY Stewart**

Indianapolis- Dec 18

The 3 bundles came this morning they are quarter stats of Fire Side sheets I have worked all day. I cannot tell how many I distributed. The weather is mild and cool, nothing new with the program.

Dec 19 (Sunday)

It was quite cold today. I did not go much out. I did not go to church.

Dec 20

I went to work bright and early today. I distributed a good many Specials. I had order from Munro to go on the same route as before down to Evansville. I will leave here about Thursday or Friday. I had no letter from home this week and I don't expect no more till I get to Louisville again.

Indianapolis- Dec 21

I have worked hard all day I canvassed a large portion of the city in the afternoon. The shoe hurted my foot very bad. I think I will leave here Friday. I had no letters today. I don't write as many letters as I used to. I am little wiser that way.

Dec 22

It is with a sad heart that I sit down to chronicle the sad news I had today that Brother Neil was drowned, Henry Soverance wrote this, "I must tell you that your brother Neil was drowned in coming from the Island the vessel struck on a reef and the captain and Cook were drowned it is in the papers". I could do nothing but weep my eyes sore in my room but alas that will do not good. I had a letter from Sarah today also written on the day as Henry S. letter and she spoke as if she did not hear a word of it as she spoke about that Neil would tell me better where he would come home and by that I knew she did not hear of it but I don't doubt of its truth for I was uneasy all along and I suspected that something was up. I am not a believer of dreams but I dreamed some time ago (sure I believe it now it was the night he was drowned) that Neil and some other fellows was on a rock and Neil I thought was making a curious kind of boat he could not get it in shape and I thought it was made of thin iron and there was a big hole on the side of the flat and they could not stop it up and when I arose in the morning I was uneasy but I tried to put it away but alas the news came. I have faint hopes yet that it may not be true as Sarah did not hear it. Alas for his poor family. I will sorely feel it too for me and him was together for a long time in Forchu and always got along well. I trust he is happier and that he wears a crown of glory now.

Dec 23 As I have been idle today waiting for the last bundle to come. I spent a sorrowful day thinking of my dear brother that I will see no more in this world but I trust I will in the next. I long to hear all about it. I am displeased with Henry Soverance to tell me at all as he did not tell me all but I fear it is too true. This is a new sorrow added to my store. I have lost my dear wife and then my little girl. I feel that I am almost as deeply wounded now, his dear little children how they will cry for their dear father who often gave them a good advice and taught them in the right path, but will never hear his voice again on the Lord's Day when he used to teach them to sing, poor big John. I feel most for him but poor Catherine will feel the stroke heavy.

Terre Haute- Dec 24.

 I left Indianapolis today at 2 pm the ? bundle did not come there when I left if it will come I left a man to distribute it C.J. W. Sheaver 65 Mass Avenue.

I have sorrowful hollow in thinking my dear brother that I will see no more. I fear at this time rolling on the bottom of the deep my heart is full. If the people around me in this Hotel only knew my feelings but little sympathy is felt here. Sometimes I can hardly make myself believe that poor Neil is drowned. I live in deep distress until I hear all about it. It is the Lord's will, he saw fit to take him from us. I hope into a better place. Poor Neil had hard trials in this world and now he is at rest. It would not be so sad if we were all around him and see him die a natural death but as will must not be done may God give us strength to bear it patiently.

Terre Haute- Dec 25.

 Many a sad thought passed through my mind today while I went about sorrowfully while others were full of glee around me. When I look back to the time some years ago when all the family lived together at home how I used to long for Christmas but of late years it brought no such yearning and this Christmas more especially for it is a sad one to all the family, his brothers (poor Neil) and sisters, but more so his poor bereaved family. May the Lord look upon them in their sore trail. But the Lord left us together a good long time and now he saw fit to cut him from our midst and if we accept and enjoy happiness from the hand of the Lord we must also take bitterness. Oh but he was taken so suddenly away. I can see him in my mind everywhere. Him and poor Bella and the baby was not far apart. I have no mind to work although I do the best I can. There is a long time since I did not drink any liquor and thoughts these was plenty around me today I did not drink any. It is more disgusting to me everyday when I see so many poor wretches drunk and murdered in every paper. I thank God that I can resist it and all the evils following it as I could not do it of my own strength. But there is plenty of evil in me besides drinking. I felt for a poor Scotchman that was in here tonight blind drunk he said he was Scotch and I think he could talk Gaelic but the landlord put him out of the hotel and scores more like him.

Terre Haute- Dec 26

Saturday night a minister came to the Hotel and gave us all a card with a cordial invitation to go to church, he was a Presbyterian. I went to his church today twice. I liked his sermon very well. His text was from Sec. Corinth 4 ch 17th verse. It suited my case very well but my mind was wandering home thinking of my bereavement when I left Forchu. The last words poor Neil said to me was to put my trust in the Lord. I try to do so but I cannot do nothing of myself. I would like to do better always. Neil always gave us all a good advice and I trust he is reaping his reward from above. They will all take his death hard but none of his brothers or sisters will take it as hard as me, they cannot, I can see him in my mind everywhere I go but that will not bring him back.

Terre Haute- Dec 27

I long to get back to Louisville for letters will be there for me. I know I would like to know the worst at once. Sometimes I will think in my mind that the Story is not true and that maybe he is still alive. It is awful to be in suspense. Why would Henry Severance say, your brother Neil was drowned and why would not Sarah tell me all and she wrote the same day? So I worked hard today to try and get away soon. I will leave here at 4:30 am tomorrow for Sullivan.

Dec 28

I came to Sullivan right early. I finished there and came to Vincennes at 8:50 pm. I need not say how I feel, I am lonesome, I am lonesome, I am weary from thinking all the time.

Princeton, Ind.- Dec 29

I came here tonight after finishing Vincennes. It was awful cold at Vincennes today the mercury was 20 deg below zero, one of my fingers got frost bitten. I have no mind to work like I used to.

Evansville Ind.- Dec 30

I got here at 11:30 am today. The weather was much warmer than yesterday. I worked pretty steady this afternoon so that I will get away tomorrow night for Louisville. I am in a hurry to get there and yet I dread to go there for I know that I will have some awful letter for me there but I must bear it with patience. The Lord will bring everything right and for his own glory.

Evansville, Ind.- Dec 31

This is the last day of the year 1880 and I have reason to be thankful that I have my health and strength but otherwise 1880 brought many a sorrow to me and more besides, but it is his own that everyone grieves for most. This time last year poor Neil's family were together and happy and then at the close of this year, Neil is taken from them and they have a sorrowful New Year. Again I was home my dear little family around me poor Bella is gone and the baby is gone but still I am thankful that dear Jonny Angus is left. Tomorrow I will hear a sad news from home. I am going to Louisville tonight. I will be there in the morning. I finished this city today. I distributed in all 6000 quarter sheets and 500 catalogues. Goodbye forever 1880 I shall never see the more.

Louisville, Ky- Jan 1, 1881

I am back to Louisville once more but I got no letter from home or from James. My anxiety is great at present but I must bear it up. I had a letter from poor Dan Ferguson, New Orleans he is well. I left Louisville last night at 6:25 pm and owing to a broken wheel of a freight car ahead we could not pass therefore it delayed us about 7 hours. I got here at 2:30 pm. I could not get the bundles to work; today the depot was closed being Holiday.

Louisville- Jan 2 Sunday

This has been a fine day I went to church today to the Broadway Tabernacle. The minister preached from the 19 chap Matthew. I spent the rest of the day in the house.

Louisville

Jan 3 I went this morning to the post office. I made sure that I would know the truth from home about Neil. When I got the letters I hated to open them for I was full of fear that the first thing would meet me was that Neil was lost-however I managed to get home to the hotel. I read them all are from poor big John and one from Sarah and Christy. They all had good hopes that Neil would soon be home but my fears are none the less.

Jan 4

I worked all the forenoon. I did not work in the afternoon it rained and sleeted. I was in the post office today and no letter. It is dreadful to be in suspense in ? and fearing the worst to come at the end such is my case. No letter from James either since I came here. I don't know what to say about it.

Jan 5

I was thinking I would get a letter from home today but none came. I am still in great suspense about Neil. It rained the latter part of this day. I had to stop at 2:30 pm. I am doing the best I can under the circumstances.

Jan 6, 1881

I am the happiest man in Louisville tonight. I cannot express how thankful I am for I got two letters this evening one from Sarah and one from AJ McAuish, St. Peters stating that Brother Neil was in Halifax all well. Now when I got these letters this evening I was afraid there was awful news. I did not read them right off for I was very nervous at last. I opened them and I fairly cried with joy. I had a fire in my room and I was all alone. Now I am going to give Henry Severance a lesson for he aught not to write me until he was sure that it was the truth.

November 6, 1880

Messrs Band and Co.

Dear Sir (this is a copy of actual letter) my object in writing to you now is to try to come to some terms to pay you for what I owe you. I don't mean to defraud you although I was compelled to leave home and am now in a strange country. Now I have to say that my wife died in June last - after being sick for two years. So I had to break up house keeping, as I went in debt a good deal during them years and I was failing in everything I tried to do. So I left with the intention of doing better here if I can. You know yourself how the world has gone against us lately. Me and Neil was fishing the first two months and did not do anything and the debtors did not pay any thing neither. I understand he had to leave home too to try to support his family and as all other hopes are gone by which I would pay you, but with my own labour will do all in my power to do so. If you will compromise with me I will pay you 50 per cent or 50 cents on the dollar for the principal only in two instalments of equal sums, one paid six months after this date and the next-one year after this date. That is the best I can do and if you will take that and give me receipt in full when the last note is paid. I will do all in my power to do it. I am canvassing for a paper in Indiana and Kentucky. Write soon so that I will be making preparations for what I said. Send me through address Donald J Stewart, Louisville, Ky Case Kitch Hotel, 48 Cast Market SL

November 15, 1880

Messrs Band and Co.

Dear Sir:

I received your letter of the 10 an hour ago. I had no idea the sum was that much when the interest was taken off. If the principle is that much $250 it is no use for me to promise on signed notes to pay in two terms on small wages and support myself and little boy. Besides you know although you have my name down for those things, that Neil was to pay as well as me. Now since I wrote you I heard from home that all the property at Forchu was to be sold at auction by the Sheriff on the first day of Dec. that comes pretty hard on me for all I had in the world was invested in those buildings which throws me out of house and home. I don't make a pitiable sum so that I would be pitier, for such has been the lot of a good many of higher means than me. If part of the proceeds went to pay your debt- I would not say a word, do not take me as a swindler although I want to compound with you for if I wanted to swindle you I need never pay you as now I have nothing but my body. But under the Act strike off the intend and I will pay half the principal as I saw in my first letter, but if it is higher than $100 I cannot pay in two terms of equal sums at 6 and 12 months, please make it this way. (as I don't want to sign but what I will pay sure if nothing happens) $40.00 6 mos after date $40.00 12 ms after date and the balance in any six months after that and I will sign notes and return, but if luck will favour me I shall not wait for the last note to come due before I pay it. Receipt in full to be given in payment of last note don't forget to serve me the account from first to last as I will sign no notes until I see it. So then the sum I will sign will be correct. Write to me soon as possible. I will be here about 10 days yet and then I am going to Indiana again. Address here ? Case of Kitch Hotel Louisville, Ky DY Stewart

Reply of letter

Mr. George Munro dear sir -- I went this morning to the post office with full assurance that instructions what to do and money was awaiting me there but was disappointed. I have used the $20 you sent me in letter dated Aug 27, very carefully. If I don't get money from you by tomorrow I will be in a strait. What to do, for I have nothing to pay my board, not that I wish in my shape to lay idle and board for I would sooner work. Send money soon as possible. DY Stewart

Copy of Telegram sent to Munro from Louisville, Ky. Sept 13

Telegram shown post marked office mistake registered letter sent Indianapolis Telegraphed for DY Stewart. Not sent

AMERICAN WOMEN'S
DIME NOVEL PROJECT

Dime Novels for Women, 1870-1920

George Munro [1864-1893]

Also known as:

Irwin Beadle & Company
George Munro & Company

George Munro was a successful publisher of cheap fiction whose firm operated from 1865 to 1893. Munro was born in Nova Scotia, Canada, on November 12, 1825. His first career plans were directed at scholarship and teaching. He studied theology and taught mathematics from 1850 to 1856 at the Free Church College in Halifax, N.S. Though trained as a minister, he never served as one. Instead, in 1856 he moved to New York City where he was employed by the American News Company and next by Beadle and Adams. In 1863, he left Beadle and Adams with Irwin Beadle to create Irwin Beadle and Company. Irwin, who had a history of irregular employment, left the firm in 1864 and the firm was renamed George Munro and Company. In 1868 the firm was renamed again, this time to simply George Munro and it would so remain until Munro retired in 1893. For the entire history of the firm, it conducted business in New York City.

In 1867 Munro introduced *The Fireside Companion*, an inexpensive story paper aimed at all members of the family. This was a successful publication and circulation grew until it reached 250,000 in 1883 (Shove, 57). *The Seaside Library*, his most successful publishing venture was introduced in 1877. The first titles in the series were English classics such as *Jane Eyre*, *Adam Bede*, and *The Last Days of Pompeii*, but he did not maintain this highbrow tone for long. Eventually the library included all of the most popular writers of sensational women's fiction such as Mary Elizabeth Braddon, Charlotte Breame, and her American "counterpart" Bertha Clay.

Despite the fact that Munro was not technically a dime novel publisher, for many of his series, such as *The Seaside Library*, sold for twenty and twenty-five cents per copy (Shove, 63), he was a resounding success in the field of cheap publishing. The popularity of *The Fireside Series* was so phenomenal that by 1879 the series contained 560 titles and sales were reported to be five and one half million copies (Shove, 61). These great sales would not remain unchallenged and eventually other

publishers would introduce "libraries" of cheap books sold in a
series. Editors at *Publishers' Weekly* noted that his activities
had:

> Affected the book publishing business in this country to
> an extraordinary extent. The people now buy nearly all
> their light reading, and that is about three quarters of what
> they read, in the form of reprints, which are sold at prices
> not much above those of newspapers...Foreign stories
> could not be sold, as before, for fifty and seventy-five cents,
> but must be put on the market for ten and twenty cents"
> (*Publishers' Weekly*, September 23, 1882: 432).

The difficulty of categorizing cheap fiction by price alone is
heightened by the attempts of cheap publishers to reach out for
better off consumers. George Munro often republished his
Seaside Library titles in cloth-bound versions for fifty cents.
And eventually, in 1887, he cut the price of his paper bound
editions from twenty and twenty-five cents to ten cents in
response to the intense competition (Shove, 63).

One of Munro's first attempts to reach women in the cheap
fiction market was his *New York Fashion Bazaar* which
appeared November 8, 1879 and featured the story, *The
Romance of Darkecliffe Hall; or, The Story of My Life* on the
front cover. The price for each issue was five cents. Based on
its appearance, it seemed that Munro intended his publication
to compete with other middle-class periodicals aimed at
women, but his choice of editor, Laura Jean Libbey, suggests
that he hoped for a working-class audience. Libbey edited the
magazine from 1891 to 1894 and received $10,400 a year for
this position, a substantial salary by any standard, particularly
for a woman (Walcutt, 403). Despite this investment in one of
the most popular cheap fiction authors of the day, Munro's
publication ceased in 1894. This was his only serious attempt to
reach women by the time he retired in 1893 he had never made
a substantial contribution to the genre.

Munro remained active in the business almost thirty years. He
retired in April 1893, just a month before the great financial
panic of 1893. Upon his death in 1896 at Pine Hill, his country
home in the Catskill Mountains, he was reputed to have an
estate worth ten million dollars. This figure may be
exaggerated, but it demonstrates that Munro hit a chord with
his cheap books and that his firm served millions of eager
readers. He was buried in Greenwood Cemetery in Brooklyn,
New York.

For details on the women's series published by George Munro,
please continue on to the George Munro section in Women's

Item Display

MUNRO, GEORGE, educator, publisher, and philanthropist; b. 12 Nov. 1825 in Millbrook, near Pictou, N.S., son of John Munro and Mary Mathieson; m. first 12 July 1855 Rachael (Rachel) Warren in Halifax, and they had a son; m. there secondly 14 Sept. 1864 Catherine Forrest, and they had a son and two daughters; d. 23 April 1896 at his summer home in the Catskills, N.Y.

One of ten children of a farmer, George Munro was apprenticed to the printing trade at the age of 12, probably in Pictou. After two years he left to further his education, first in New Glasgow and then, after supporting himself with teaching jobs for several years, at Pictou Academy between 1844 and 1847. On graduation he again taught school in New Glasgow, before becoming an instructor in mathematics and natural philosophy at Free Church Academy, Halifax, in 1850. Two years later he was appointed rector (principal). Although he prepared himself for the Presbyterian ministry and was highly regarded as a teacher, he resigned from the academy in 1856. Abandoning his clerical ambitions, he left Nova Scotia, for reasons of health according to his own account, and settled in New York City.

In New York this Nova Scotian Horatio Alger began his journey from teacher to millionaire businessman by returning to the printing and publishing business. He worked first for D. Appleton and Company, where, according to an advertisement that appeared in the Halifax papers in 1861, he was involved in mail order and distribution for British magazines and books. In 1862 he moved to Ross and Tousey, then a year later to Beadle and Company, a pioneer in the production of cheap books. He left this firm in 1866 and, after a short-lived partnership with Irwin Beadle, soon struck out on his own with the publication of the *Fireside Companion* (later the *New York Fireside Companion*), a weekly family paper which would absorb his energies for the next ten years. The *Fireside Companion* found both readers and contributors in Nova Scotia, where Munro returned for frequent visits after his second marriage in 1864. In 1877 he started a series of reprints of modern English works called the Seaside Library in imitation of the Lakeside Library published by Donnelley, Lloyd and Company. It soon included fiction, history, biography, travel, and religious works, eventually comprising more than a thousand titles. In the absence of international copyright laws Munro, like his contemporaries, did not pay royalties to authors or permission fees to original publishers. As a result he was able to provide high-quality literature cheaply to North American readers. He amassed considerable capital, which he invested in a large printing plant and in the acquisition and development of New York real estate.

By the 1870s Munro was a rich man and could have bought the best education for his children, but it was presumably his continued attachment to Nova Scotia that prompted him in 1874 to send his 14-year-old son, George William, to Dalhousie College in Halifax. A non-sectarian, but basically Presbyterian postsecondary institution, Dalhousie had operated continuously only since 1863. In 1878, the year of George William Munro's graduation, the college had an enrolment of 93 men and a teaching staff of 10. It was nearing the end of a five-year government grant and participation in the short-lived University of Halifax, an examining body for all provincially supported colleges in Nova Scotia modelled after the University of London. Faced with the imminent reduction of the government grant, which accounted for almost half of its income, and unable to pay competitive salaries for high-quality staff, the college was on the brink of collapse. During a holiday in Nova Scotia in 1879, Munro was alerted to the perilous condition of the college by his wife's brother, John Forrest*, minister of St John's Church in Halifax and the Presbyterian synod's recent appointee to the Dalhousie board of governors.

The college's predicament struck a responsive chord in George Munro. Over the next six years, until his younger son, John, matriculated at Dalhousie in 1885, the publisher donated more than $300,000 to establish chairs and to provide a short-term program of tutorships and scholarships. John Munro thus studied at an institution where 7 of the 20 faculty members and 50 of the 163 students were supported by his father's liberality. Munro endowed chairs of physics in 1879, history and political economy in 1880, English literature and philosophy in 1882, constitutional and international law in 1883, and a separate chair of English in 1884. The salaries attached to these five chairs, ranging from $2,000 to $2,500, doubled professorial incomes and raised the professoriate, perhaps unwisely, to a standard of living comparable to that of the social élite. In the short term, however, the chairs attracted several of the region's most able young academics, men such as James Gordon MacGregor* in physics and Jacob Gould Schurman in philosophy. The endowment of the chair in law resulted in the founding of the Dalhousie law school, the first academic institution in Canada whose teaching was based on the common law [see Sir John Sparrow David THOMPSON].

The tutorships demonstrated the gap between Munro's expectations for Dalhousie and local realities. They were essentially remedial teaching positions designed to bring students from the weaker high schools up to the level of their better-educated peers from Pictou Academy, Halifax Academy, and Charlottetown's Prince of Wales College. The program of exhibitions and bursaries, amounting to nearly $85,000 and awarded on the basis of examinations, was also "so offered for competition as to stimulate to greater activity and efficiency the High Schools and Academies of Nova Scotia and the neighbouring Provinces." Given the numerous occasions on which no scholarships were awarded, Munro's concern for the quality of secondary education appears to have been amply justified. None the less, these scholarships enabled the first two women to enter the undergraduate program in 1881 and supported more than half of the first 25 female graduates of Dalhousie. Munro also donated books and journal subscriptions, not only to the college library, but also to the Citizens' Free Library in Halifax and the reading-room of the Amalgamated Trades Union.

Munro restrained himself from exercising undue patronage in conjunction with his gifts. Admittedly he appointed his brother-in-law, John Forrest, to the most generously endowed chair, that in history and political economy, and he named individuals to the board of governors, as his donations legally entitled him to do. He refused himself to become a member of the board, preferring that kind of activity closer to home in the University of the City of New York. But with Forrest as Dalhousie's president from 1885, Munro's wishes were not in danger of being overlooked. In any case, he had ceased by the mid 1880s to add to his gifts, although he continued to meet his earlier obligations with quarterly payments until 1893, when a trust fund was established. He left the college no further bequests in his will; however, the board of governors successfully made a claim against the estate that added another $82,000 to the George Munro Trust Fund.

Munro's vital contribution to the welfare of Dalhousie was recognized in 1881 by the creation of a college holiday in his honour, an event that continues to this day. Munro was Dalhousie's first major benefactor and the most generous donor to a Canadian university in the 19th century. Arguably Munro's gifts to Dalhousie changed the whole course of university education in Nova Scotia. If the college had been allowed to collapse, as seemed likely in the late 1870s, politicians and educational administrators might have been forced finally to consolidate the various colleges in the province into a single university. As it was, Munro's gifts gave Dalhousie a degree of independence that not only helped to increase its enrolment and to improve the quality of its faculty but also enabled it to begin its transformation into a full-fledged university through the establishment of professional schools. In a sense, then, the Munro endowment was a mixed blessing. Munro's generosity did little, moreover, to stem the tide of migration of talented people from the Maritimes. Those who left were better educated, and they included some of Dalhousie's most able students and its most brilliant faculty members. Munro's own son-in-law, J. G. Schurman, left Halifax in 1886 for Cornell University, where he became president. Munro himself was a precursor of the later exodus, and his success demonstrated why human resources had become the most important export from the Maritimes by the late 19th century. But Munro, like Izaak Walton Killam* and Sir James Hamet Dunn* in the 20th century, returned with generous interest the investment his native province had made in him.

JUDITH FINGARD

[The records of Dalhousie Univ. (Halifax) in the university's archives are very disappointing as a source of information on Munro. According to the archivist, most of the correspondence and papers pertaining to the president's office before 1911 were destroyed in the 1930s. J.F.]

DUA, MS 1-1, A, 1879–1901; B, George Munro letters, 27 Jan. 1881; 11 Oct., 1 Nov. 1884; 30 March 1889; MS 1-6, cash-books and ledgers, 1879–1900; George Munro letters, 26 March, 27 Dec. 1887; MS 1–7, matriculation and registration books, 1874–98. PANS, RG 32, M, 189, no.26; WB, 65, no.150. Memorial of George Munro, born November 12, 1825, died April 25, 1896 (New York, 1896). Dalhousie Gazette (Halifax), 15 Nov. 1879; 18 Nov. 1880; 11, 25 Nov. 1881; 3 May 1882; 13 Jan., 23 Nov., 24 Dec. 1883; 14 Feb., 30 April, 10 Nov. 1884; 23 Jan., 6 Feb., 4 May, 14 Nov. 1885; 16 Jan., 15 Dec. 1886; 23 April 1887; 31 Jan. 1889; 20 Dec. 1893; 11 May 1896. Halifax Herald, 8 Sept. 1894; 24, 29 April, 5–6 May 1896. Morning Chronicle (Halifax), 22 Aug. 1879; 3 Nov. 1880; 26 Oct. 1881; 10 June 1882; 25 Jan., 14 Feb., 10 Aug. 1883; 24 Jan., 9, 12 Feb., 5 April, 31 July 1884; 30 June 1885; 5–6 Feb. 1886; 29 April 1896. Morning Herald (Halifax), 27 April 1887, 2 Feb. 1889, 14 Jan. 1891. New-York Times, 25 April, 5 May 1896. Novascotian, 11 Oct. 1851, 19 July 1852, 24 Jan. 1853, 8 April 1854. Presbyterian Witness, and Evangelical Advocate, 11 Oct. 1851, 8 April 1854, 23 Oct. 1856, 5 Oct. 1861. Belcher's farmer's almanack, 1853–57. DAB. Dalhousie College and Univ., Calendar (Halifax), 1874/75–1899/1900. A. E. Marble, Nova Scotians at home and abroad, including brief biographical sketches of over six hundred native born Nova Scotians (Windsor, N.S., 1977). P. R. Blakeley, Glimpses of Halifax, 1867–1900 (Halifax, 1949; repr. Belleville, Ont., 1973). J. G. Reid, Mount Allison University: a history, to 1963 (2v., Toronto, 1984), 1. Waite, Man from Halifax. John Willis, A history of Dalhousie Law School (Toronto, 1979). A. J. Crockett, "George Munro, 'The Publisher,'" Dalhousie Rev., 35 (1955–56): 328–38; 36 (1956–57): 69–83, 163–73, 279–85; reissued in book form in a limited edition (Halifax, 1957). D. C. Harvey, "The Dalhousie idea," "The early struggles of Dalhousie," "From college to university," and "Dalhousie University established," Dalhousie Rev., 17 (1937–38): 131–43, 311–26, 411–31, and 18 (1938–39): 50–66; repub. as An introduction to the history of Dalhousie University (Halifax, 1938).

www.ingramcontent.com/pod-product-compliance
Lightning Source LLC
Chambersburg PA
CBHW030914260626
47169CB00008B/2835

*9 7 8 3 3 3 7 3 0 0 4 5 6 *